MW00912484

Mysteries
OF THE
OCEAN DEEP

© Aladdin Books Ltd 1996

Designed and produced by
Aladdin Books Ltd
28 Percy Street
London W1P 0LD

First published in the United States in 1996 by
Copper Beech Books,
an imprint of the Millbrook Press
2 Old New Milford Road
Brookfield, Connecticut 06804

Consultant: Dr. David George

Editor: Katie Roden
Design:
David West Children's Book Design
Designer: Edward Simkins
Picture Research: Brooks Krikler Research
Illustrators: Francis Phillipps; Rob Shone; Gary Slater, Simon Girling & Associates

Printed in Belgium

Library of Congress Cataloging-in-Publication Data

Dipper, Frances, 1951-
The ocean deep / by Frances Dipper :
illustrated by Simon Girling & Associates.
p. cm. -- (Mysteries of --)
Includes index.
ISBN 0-7613-0454-1 (lib. bdg.). --
ISBN 0-7613-0469-X (pbk.)
1. Oceanography--Juvenile literature.
[1. Oceanography. 2. Ocean.]
I. Simon Girling & Associates.
II. Title. III. Series.
GC21.5.D56 1996   95-40835
551.46--dc20   CIP
                                              AC

Mysteries
OF THE
OCEAN DEEP

Dr. Frances Dipper

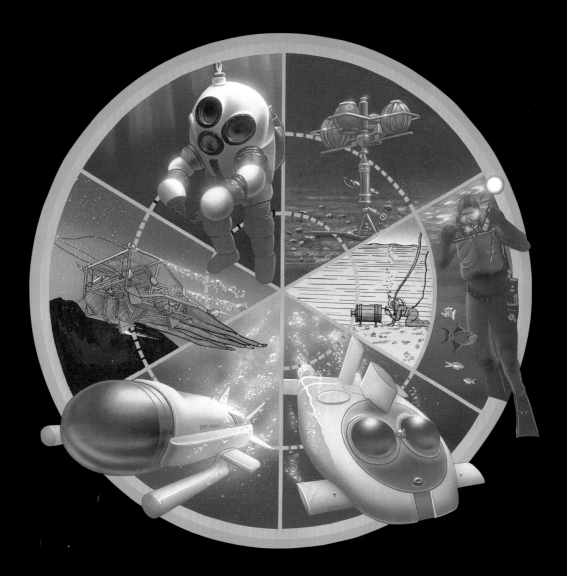

Copper Beech Books
Brookfield, Connecticut

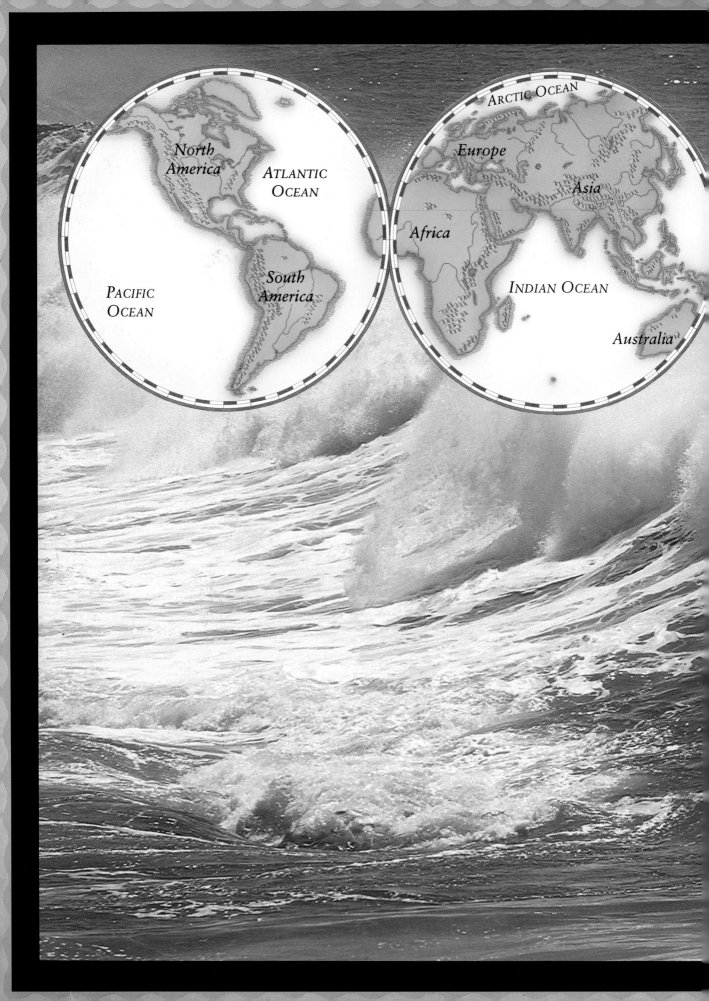

CONTENTS

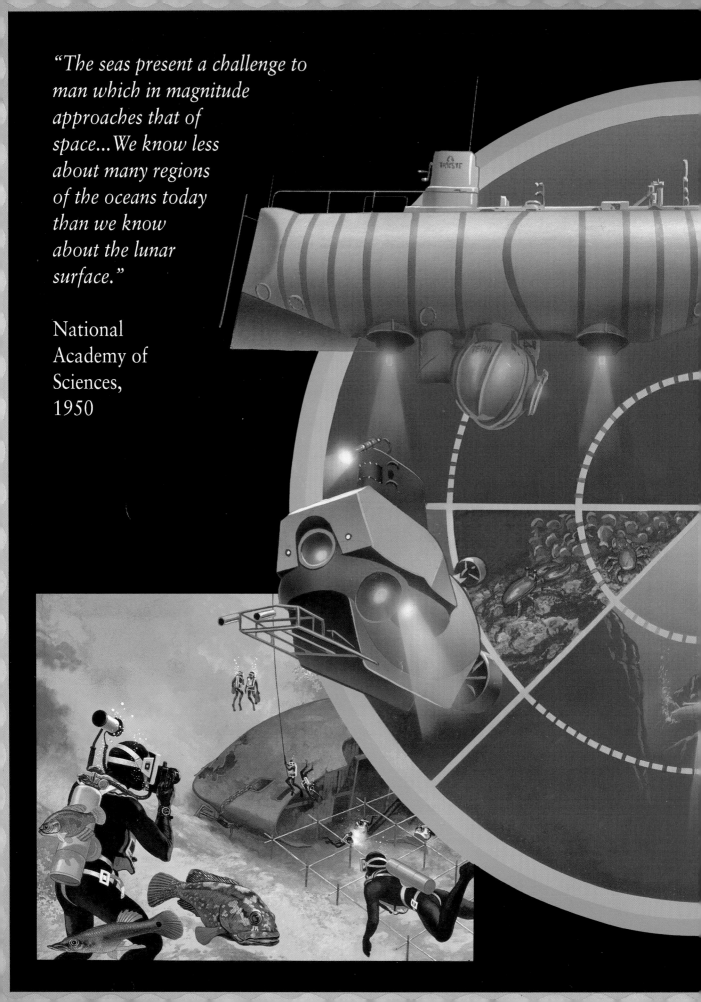

"*The seas present a challenge to man which in magnitude approaches that of space...We know less about many regions of the oceans today than we know about the lunar surface.*"

National Academy of Sciences, 1950

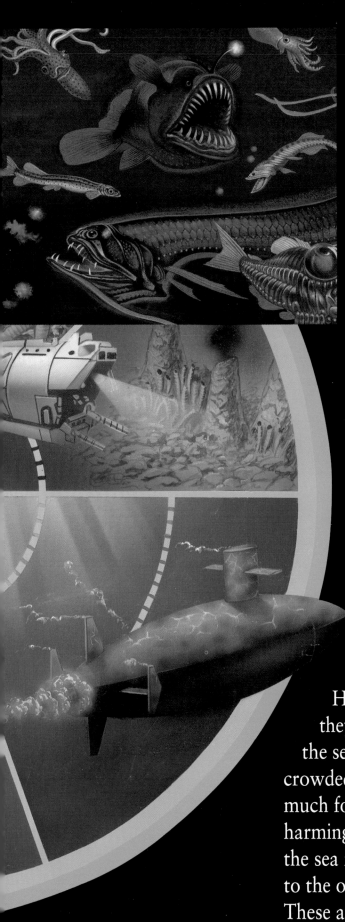

Introduction to
THE MYSTERIES

Perhaps our world should have been called "Planet Ocean" and not "Planet Earth." After all, more than two-thirds of its surface is covered by water. Scientists have worked out that the oceans contain about 529 million cubic miles of water! That's a lot of ocean to explore.

When Neil Armstrong stood on the Moon in 1969, only one successful mission had ever been made to the deepest part of the oceans. No one has returned there since. The secrets of the ocean depths are not easy to solve, but many people have been willing to try. In the 20th century, huge advances have been made in the development of exploration methods, but many questions remain. How did the oceans form and why are they so salty? Will people ever live under the sea? As our world becomes more crowded, we must understand our oceans. How much food can we take from the sea without harming it? How can we use our wastes to feed the sea rather than pollute it? What will happen to the oceans if "global warming" continues? These are just some of the many questions and mysteries facing today's marine scientists.

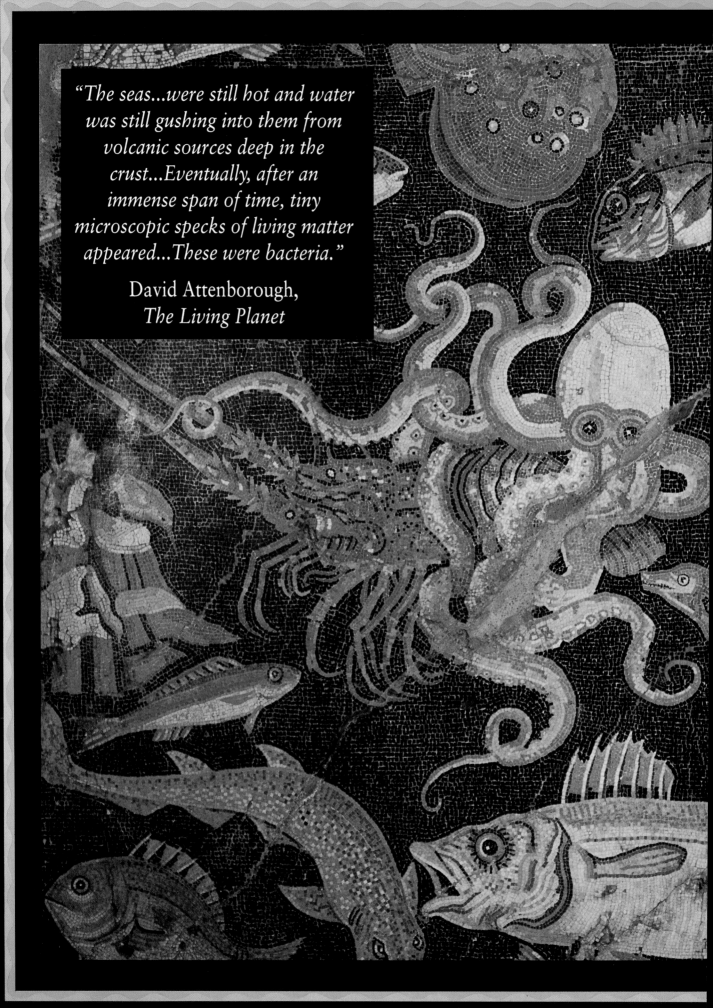

"*The seas...were still hot and water was still gushing into them from volcanic sources deep in the crust...Eventually, after an immense span of time, tiny microscopic specks of living matter appeared...These were bacteria.*"

David Attenborough,
The Living Planet

The Mysterious
WATERS

Today, thanks to underwater video cameras, people can travel the oceans without even getting wet. Modern ships, submarines, diving equipment, and satellite technology allow us to see into and explore the ocean's depths.

Early explorers braved the oceans with no real maps or communications systems. The Romans were accurate observers, as we know from their mosaics of Mediterranean fish and other sea creatures.

Until about 150 years ago, scientists believed that nothing could live in the deepest depths of the oceans, and that the deep seabed was covered in ice. But in 1860, a communications cable that ran under the Mediterranean Sea, at a depth of 1.3 miles (2 km), was brought to the surface for repairs. Growing on it were beautiful deep-sea corals. In modern times, deep-sea dredges have brought up a variety of ocean creatures from as far below the surface as 3.8 miles (6 km).

The First
MYSTERIES

FIRST PAST THE POST
In 1773, Constantine John Phipps used a weighted line to measure a depth of over 0.6 miles (1 km) in the waters between Iceland and Norway, from his ship, H.M.S Racehorse.

Until two centuries ago, people believed that the oceans were bottomless and full of huge, hideous monsters. In the 18th century, however, scientists and explorers began to carry out experiments which helped them to find the bottom of the ocean.

Since 1920, scientists have used echo sounders to measure depth anywhere in the ocean in a matter of seconds and to show them what the seabed looks like. Divers can even carry their own small, waterproof echo sounders to tell them how far above the seabed they are. Even so, many mysteries and myths remain.

How big are the oceans?
Seas and oceans cover about 140,000,000 sq miles (362,000,000 sq km) of our planet, with an average depth of 2.3 miles (3.7 km). The biggest ocean is the Pacific, which measures 64,000,000 sq miles (166,000,000 sq km); the smallest is the Arctic Ocean, at 4,600,000 sq miles (12,000,000 sq km).

MAGICAL MERMAIDS
No one knows how the legends of mermaids began, but they have been told for centuries. The Spanish explorer Christopher Columbus (1451–1506) thought dugongs or sea cows (right) may have inspired the myth.

LIFE IN THE DEPTHS?

Scientists now know that life can exist on the seabed even in the deepest part of the ocean, the Mariana Trench. This was examined in 1995 by Kaiko (left), a Japanese crewless submarine. It is operated by cables from the surface and has brought back samples and pictures.

THE CHALLENGE OF THE OCEANS

In 1872, H.M.S. Challenger set off on a worldwide voyage of scientific research. For over three years, the ship's scientists mapped the seabed by taking depth soundings using a line and a lead ball. They tested mud and water and found over 4,000 new species of animals and plants. Their work filled 50 books and solved many mysteries.

Gods of the sea

Seafaring peoples have worshiped sea gods and goddesses for thousands of years. Rituals and ceremonies to please such gods are still practiced in some cultures today. Each major civilization had sea gods, such as Poseidon in ancient Greece and the Roman god Neptune (right). The crests on waves were believed by the Romans to be the white horses that pulled Neptune's chariot (top).

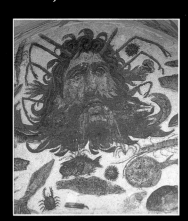

WHIRLING WATERS

Whirlpools form where strong tidal currents meet in narrow stretches of water, such as between Italy and Sicily in the Mediterranean Sea. Ancient Greek sailors called this whirlpool Charybdis *and thought it was caused by a monster sucking in and spitting out the water.*

THE LOST ISLAND

Even today no one knows if the continent of Atlantis ever existed. The ancient Greek writer Plato described a mythical island that was engulfed by waves. In about 1500 B.C., a volcanic eruption and earthquake on the island of Thira (now Santorini) had caused tidal waves and flooding. This event may have started the legend.

Changing VIEWS

The early explorers of the oceans must have been very brave. They had ships powered only by sails, and navigated using the stars and the Sun. They had no accurate maps and some believed that they might fall off the edge of the world. Explorers like Christopher Columbus, Ferdinand Magellan, and James Cook mapped out the ocean surfaces and the continents. Now scientists are starting to chart the world of mountains, trenches, and plains deep beneath the oceans. By drilling into the seabed, they are even able to work out how the oceans and continents were formed and where they will be in a million years!

Do the oceans stay the same size?
The size of our oceans is changing all the time, because of the constant, slow movements of the Earth's tectonic plates (see page 13) which pull the continents apart. For example, the Atlantic Ocean grows about 1.6 in (4 cm) wider every year. Other oceans and seas are widening very gradually, for the same reasons.

THE FLAT EARTH

For many centuries, people thought the Earth was flat and they could fall off the edge! In the 6th century B.C., the Greek mathematician Pythagoras (below) proved that the Earth was a sphere. Satellite pictures now allow us to look at our spherical world. But some people still insist that it is flat!

THE FIRST AROUND-
THE-WORLD VOYAGE,
1522

FINDING A LINK

The Portuguese sailor Ferdinand Magellan crossed the Pacific Ocean in 1520. Before this, people had thought that India and America were joined by land. In 1522, one of his ships was the first to sail around the world, finally proving that the Earth was spherical.

MAPPING THE WORLD
Some ancient peoples had strange ideas about the Earth's shape! In about A.D. 50, Pomponius Mela from Rome drew a "wheel map" of a flat Earth surrounded by an ocean and divided by seas.

OCEAN SPINES
The Atlantic Ocean covers the Mid-Atlantic Ridge, a long chain of mountains up to 7.6 miles (4 km) high. It juts out in places to form islands like Iceland. There are ridges like this under all the oceans.

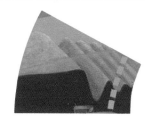

DRILLING DEEP
The Glomar Challenger *(left) has helped to solve the mystery of how the ocean floor was formed and how old it is. A drill digs into the seabed to collect samples of rock and silt. It can work in water up to 4.5 miles (7 km) deep.*

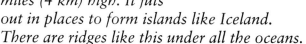

THE WHOLE PICTURE
The first world atlas, Theatrum Orbis Terrarum, *was published in 1570 by a Flemish map-maker, Abraham Ortelius. It contained maps which had been specially drawn for the book. It was very popular, but very inaccurate!*

The changing Earth
Scientists now believe that the oceans and continents sit on separate pieces, or tectonic plates (below), of the Earth's outer crust. About 250 million years ago, the continents were all joined together in a vast landmass known as *Pangaea*. Many plates have gradually pulled apart, moving the continents. They are still moving today. Some of the plates have collided, pushing up mountain ranges like the Himalayas.

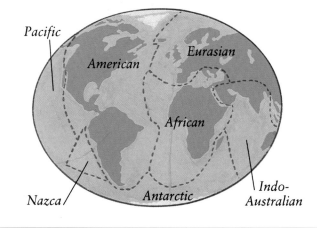

Pacific

American

Eurasian

African

Nazca

Antarctic

Indo-Australian

"I experimented with all possible maneuvers of the Aqua-Lung: loops, somersaults and barrel rolls. I stood upside down on one finger and burst out laughing – a shrill, distorted laugh...Delivered from gravity and buoyancy, I flew around in space..."

Jacques Cousteau, underwater explorer

The Lure of the
OCEANS

Most of us are fascinated by the ocean. For thousands of years, fishermen, coastal peoples, and seafarers have made their living from it and have had ways of life that revolve around it. Many people visit it on vacation for a few weeks each year. Others venture into it in search of pearls and other natural treasures.

By the 19th century, natural history had become popular. Early naturalists began to explore the mysterious animals and plants of the seashore. Some even ventured a short way underwater with buckets over their heads! Marine laboratories were built next to the sea in places like Naples in Italy and Plymouth in England. After World War II (1939–1945), underwater explorers, like Hans and Lottie Hass from Austria and Jacques Cousteau from France, began to take pictures of the strange worlds found beyond the seashore. Today, there are many underwater expeditions, which find more and more mysterious creatures every year.

The First DIVERS

People have been diving in the sea for thousands of years, to search for valuable sponges and pearls or fish and other food. The earliest divers had no equipment, but with practice could dive to 60–100 feet (20–30 m) while holding their breath. As the centuries passed, curiosity and the hope of finding treasure or defeating enemies led to the development of all kinds of diving aids. Even the Italian artist and inventor Leonardo da Vinci (1452–1519) designed a device for breathing underwater, although he never tried it. Today, thousands of people enjoy diving as a sport.

Where do pearls come from?
A pearl is formed when an irritating particle of sand gets into a shell. It is covered in smooth *nacre* (mother-of-pearl) to stop the itch. Many shellfish can form pearls, but valuable pearls come only from tropical seas. The biggest pearl ever found weighs over 13 lb (6 kg) and came from a giant clam.

JEWELS OF
THE SEA
Some of the first human divers were pearl and sponge collectors. Pearls have been gathered in the Arabian Gulf since at least 3000 B.C. Early divers wore tortoise-shell nose clips to keep water out of their nostrils.

UNDER THE SEAS

The astronomer Edmund Halley invented the first diving bell in 1690. Divers sat in a wooden cask with an open bottom. As the cask was lowered, the air inside was squashed by the rising water, so extra air was pumped in from wooden barrels. Divers could walk outside the bell with small casks over their heads.

THE HELMET SUIT

The first diving suit was developed in 1837 by Augustus Siebe from Germany. The watertight rubber suit had a heavy copper helmet which kept the diver on the seabed. Air was pumped down from the surface. This allowed divers to work at over 300 feet (90 m) deep. A very similar but lighter suit is now used by commercial divers.

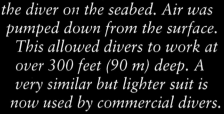

Getting the bends

Early divers suffered from a strange, often fatal disease – decompression sickness, or the bends. If divers surface too fast, the decrease in pressure makes the nitrogen gas in their blood form bubbles, which block the blood's flow. Dive computers can work out the safest ascent speed. Divers with the bends go into decompression chambers (right), with high air pressure to make the gas dissolve.

DIVING ALONE

In 1865, Benoît Rouquayrol and Auguste Denayrouze invented a diving set that did not need an air hose from the surface. Air was carried in a canister and fed through a valve in the helmet. But the set could be used only in shallow water at low pressure.

DIVING TODAY

Modern SCUBA (Self-Contained Underwater Breathing Apparatus) gives divers great freedom. The Aqua-Lung, the first breathing device to let people dive independently, was invented in the 1940s. The explorers Jacques Cousteau and Frédéric Dumas developed the demand valve, which gives air to divers when they breathe in (rather than all the time, which wastes air).

Mysterious CREATURES

The number of sea creatures roaming the seas is truly amazing. Among the most spectacular ocean dwellers are the great whales, sharks, and manta rays. In the past, they were seen only as a source of food and money and many were hunted and killed. Now scientists are trying to unravel the mysterious lives of these enormous creatures, in the hope of saving them from extinction.

Today, it is possible for everyone to see some of these amazing animals in the wild. Many travel agencies now offer whale and dolphin watching trips, coral-reef safaris, and trips in glass-bottomed boats, while more and more people are learning to scuba dive.

MONSTERS OF THE DEEP
Early seafarers lived in constant fear of the hideous monsters that were believed to lurk in the ocean. Sixteenth-century books and maps show fish and reptiles with huge heads and fangs and long, writhing serpents. Such beliefs persisted well into the 19th century.

Ruler of the seas
The blue whale is the largest animal on Earth. It can grow up to 100 feet (30 m) long – bigger than most of the dinosaurs. Yet this giant mammal eats shrimps called *krill* that are just 2 in (5 cm) long. Each whale swallows about 4 million krill every day!

SHARK ATTACK!

Films like Jaws *have given the great white shark a reputation as a terrifying killer. With its huge jaws and sharp teeth, it can tear a person apart. Little is known about the life of this monster and scientists are trying to find out more. But people have killed more sharks than sharks have killed people – and this huge predator is now an endangered species.*

How great is the great white shark? Most great white sharks can grow to more than 20 feet (6 m) long. In 1959, Alfred Dean caught the largest fish ever taken with a rod, off the coast of Australia. It was a great white weighing 664 lb (1,209.5 kg). The biggest great white ever caught was also caught off the Australian coast, in 1976, by Clive Green. It weighed 3,338 lb (1,537 kg). Australian Rodney Fox survived a great white shark attack in 1963. He had hundreds of stitches and still has scars from his waist to his neck.

LARVAE ALERT

In 1763, leaf-shaped fish were found in the Sargasso Sea and named Leptocephalus. A century later, it was proved that they were young freshwater eels. The eels lay their eggs in the sea, and the larvae travel to North America and Europe, where they swim into rivers.

MEGALODON

GREAT WHITE

DEADLY GIANTS

Early Mediterranean peoples believed that fossilized sharks' teeth were snakes' tongues, turned to stone when St. Paul visited Malta in A.D. 60. *Some teeth are 5 in (12 cm) long and suggest a huge, extinct shark, Megalodon, which could have been 100 feet (30 m) long!*

THE DEVIL'S CREATURES

The strange "horns" on the manta ray's head have earned it the name of "devil-fish." Until the 1920s, it was thought to be a dangerous predator. Divers now swim happily with

these giants. Despite its huge size, the manta feeds only on floating plankton (tiny organisms). The "horns" help to direct plankton-rich water into its mouth.

"Now and then I felt a slight vibration and
an apparent slackening off of the cable.
Word came that a cross-swell had
arisen...We were swinging at 3,028 feet,
and, would we come up?"

William Beebe, on his record bathysphere
descent in 1934

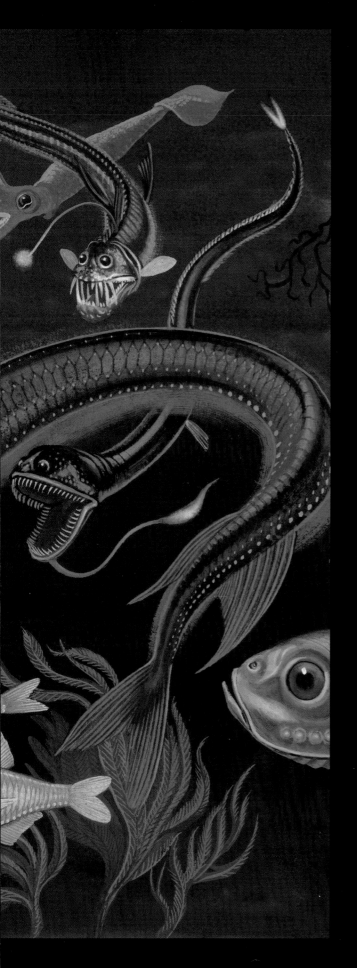

The Deepest DEPTHS

A thousand yards down in the ocean depths, the sea is icy cold. It is pitch black and the water pressure is strong enough to crush a person like an eggshell. These are the problems faced both by underwater explorers and by the animals that live here.

The animals solve such problems in ingenious ways. Most deep-sea fish have luminous body parts with which to hunt and find mates. Some squid even squirt luminous "ink" (fluid) to confuse predators. Food is scarce in the depths; most fish have huge jaws and expandable stomachs and can eat prey which is at least as big as they are. The males of some species are attached to the females, to make sure the females have mates.

The explorers are protected by submersibles (submarines) made from strong materials. They carry food and water and are well heated. They also have powerful lights so that the crew can see the water around them.

Ocean Trenches & VENTS

HITTING THE BOTTOM
On January 23, 1960, Navy Lt. Donald Walsh and Jacques Piccard dived into the ocean's deepest trench, the Mariana, in the bathyscaph Trieste. They reached the bottom over 4 hours later, after traveling nearly 7 miles (11 km).

Like the urge to climb the highest mountains on Earth, people have always wanted to dive deeper and explore the "inner space" of the oceans. In the last thirty years, deep-sea research submarines have made this possible. Most of these can operate down to less than one mile deep, but much of the ocean floor lies below this. The *Trieste* voyage in 1960 is the only time people have ever descended to the deepest part of the ocean. With such submersibles, scientists have discovered underwater volcanoes, hot-water vents and many previously unimagined animals.

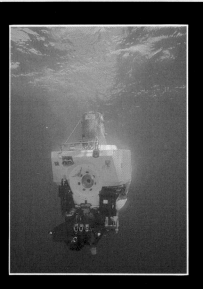

Exploring the seabed

Today, scientists can explore the deep seabed in small submersibles like the *Alvin*, built in 1964. They use instruments that measure, film, and collect the water and animals around the craft. It moves freely, but it cannot go much deeper than 2.4 miles (4 km). The *Alvin* discovered marine life around deep-sea vents (see page 23).

OASES OF LIFE

In the deep ocean, the water is icy cold. But hot springs may escape from volcanic cracks, or vents, in the seabed. In 1977, scientists explored a vent 1.3 miles (2 km) down, near the Galapagos Islands.

It was teeming with tube worms, mussels, crabs, and fish, feeding on bacteria and each other. The bacteria get their energy from the sulfurous gases and minerals that come out of the vents. So the whole food web depends on chemical energy rather than sunlight.

BLACK SMOKERS

The Nautile has found deep-sea vents near Mexico, in which tall chimneys of hardened minerals have built up. Hot water gushes out at temperatures of up to 730 °F. As it rises from the surrounding rock, the water reacts with the minerals and turns black, pouring out of the chimney like smoke.

MODERN SUBMERSIBLES

The giants of the submarine world are the nuclear craft. Small research submersibles can stay submerged for only a few days, but nuclear submarines remain underwater for up to 2 years. They are bigger than most passenger ships and carry large crews.

DEEP DOWN

The deepest spot on Earth is the 7-mile Challenger Deep in the Pacific Ocean's Mariana Trench (see page 22). The water pressure at the bottom is an astounding 1.25 tons per square yard.

Which is the highest underwater mountain? The biggest known mountain under the surface of the sea is Mount Kea, underneath the Pacific Ocean. It climbs to a massive 6 miles (10 km) above the sea floor. It is therefore almost 1.2 miles (2 km) higher than Mount Everest, the tallest mountain on land – yet it is still invisible from the surface of the ocean!

The Living
D E P T H S

One of the greatest challenges to scientists is finding out what mysterious creatures live in the depths of the oceans. Delicate animals like jellyfish simply break apart as they are hauled to the surface, because the temperature and pressure changes on the way up are too great for their fragile bodies.

In recent years, many new species have been collected using sensitive robotic arms on submersibles. With these machines, the scientists can gently place the animals in special protective containers before taking them out of the water. Finding an animal that no one has ever seen before is very exciting!

How deep can fish swim?
The deepest that a fish has been caught is at 5 miles (8 km) beneath the surface of the Atlantic Ocean. The fish was a type of eel and was caught by Dr. Gilbert L. Voss in 1970. A living creature has been seen even further down, at 7 miles (11 km) under the Pacific Ocean. It was probably a flat sea cucumber.

GIANT JAWS
"Megamouth," the most mysterious of all sharks, was first hauled up from deep water in 1976. It can be 15 feet (4.5 m) long and weighs at least 1,650 lb (750 kg). With its huge mouth and tiny teeth, it eats only small creatures.
What a relief!

CLEAN UP!
Over 0.6 miles (1 km) down in all the major oceans, there are great "deserts" of soft mud, kept clean by deep-sea vacuum cleaners! These sea cucumbers feed by sucking up mud, full of the dead remains of creatures from above.

DEEP-SEA DWELLERS
Dive deeper than about 2,000 feet (600 m) in the sea and you will find yourself in a world of darkness, broken by strange flashes of light.

Deep-sea fish carry luminous lamps on their bodies to help them hunt and catch prey. Fish of the same species can recognize each other from their particular light patterns.

A living fossil?

The coelacanth looks more like a reptile than a fish. Before 1938, only fossilized coelacanths more than 70 million years old had been found. In that year, a live specimen was caught and taken to a museum in South Africa. Sadly, this "living fossil" may soon become extinct. Only a few hundred remain, living at depths of 495–990 feet (150–300 m) near the Comoro Islands between Madagascar and Mozambique.

MYSTERIOUS HUES
Sunlight consists of rainbow colors. In water, each color only travels to a certain depth. Red stops first, so red animals look almost black in the depths. Many deep-sea creatures, like prawns (above) and sea spiders (below), are red, for camouflage in their dark world.

JELLYFISH
Many kinds of jellyfish and similar animals live in the ocean depths. Some are large, like the lion's mane jellyfish which grows to 6.6 feet (2 m) across its bell (body). Others are tiny. Many glow with bright colors as they move, and stun other creatures with stinging tentacles like those of the compass jellyfish (left).

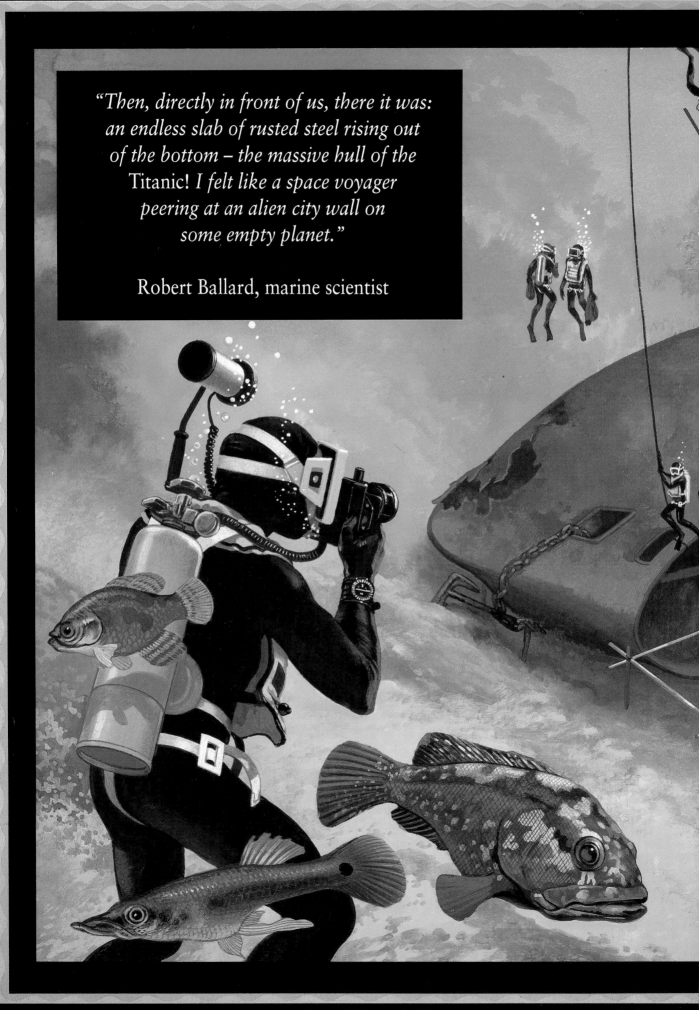

"*Then, directly in front of us, there it was: an endless slab of rusted steel rising out of the bottom – the massive hull of the Titanic! I felt like a space voyager peering at an alien city wall on some empty planet.*"

Robert Ballard, marine scientist

Treasures of THE DEEP

Over the centuries there have been many shipwrecks, and much treasure has been lost in the ocean depths. Today, with the help of technology, some of these valuables are coming to the surface again. Robot submersibles with video cameras can be sent to find treasure and to help scientists work out ways of recovering it.

Amateur divers enjoy exploring wrecks and many have helped to uncover archaeological "treasures." The famous wreck of the *Mary Rose* was recovered almost entirely by volunteers. In 1995, divers finished excavating a 3,313-year-old Bronze Age wreck in the Mediterranean Sea. Such "time capsules" have taught us a lot about our past. Wrecks can survive in the sea for thousands of years because they are preserved by mud or sand. This also makes them difficult to find! Archaeologists must dig away the sediment carefully, just as they do on land.

Underwater HUNTS

Many people dream of finding sunken treasure...but few have succeeded. Time, money, and equipment are needed to do so. However, finding treasure has been made much easier with modern technology. Once treasure is found, it is possible to go back to an exact spot in the sea using a Global Positioning System. This takes readings from satellites in space and is accurate to within a few yards.

Not all treasure is made of gold – 24,000 valuable plates were raised from a wreck called the *Diana* in 1994. The ship sank near Singapore in 1817 in only 106 feet (32 m) of water, but was quickly buried in sand.

RAISING THE PAST
The flagship of King Henry VIII of England, the Mary Rose, *was raised from the English seabed in 1982. It sank in 1545, and has told historians a lot about life in Tudor times. It was pulled up by the* Tor Mog, *the biggest lifting barge in existence.*

Liquid riches

Oil is known as the sea's "black gold." Countries like Saudi Arabia and Brunei have become rich by collecting oil from beneath their seas. Most oil rigs can work only in less than 660 feet (200 m) of water. Now special drilling ships are finding oil in much deeper places. Computers keep the ship in the right spot while it drills through the seabed.

SEARCHING FOR WRECKS

Many wrecks are found by sonar equipment (left). Waves of sound are sent to the seabed. When they bounce back, the pattern they make shows up lumps and bumps.

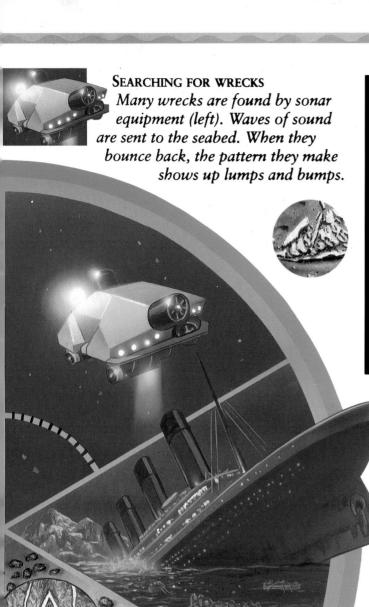

What is the oldest shipwreck?
The oldest known wreck dates from the 14th century B.C., and still lies off the coast of Turkey.
Do the oceans contain any other natural treasures?
Sea water contains tiny amounts of gold, but not enough to be extracted (unfortunately!). Other valuable elements, such as magnesium and bromine, can be taken from the water.

A TERRIBLE DISASTER

In 1912, the biggest ocean liner ever, the Titanic, *collided with an iceberg. Over 1,500 people died as the ship sank to the seabed, 2.4 miles (4 km) below. It was found in 1985 (below), using hi-tech equipment. Submersibles have since taken scientists to see the sad remains.*

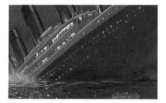

TREASURE!

In 1994, salvage expert Bob Hudson raised a haul of silver coins using a remote-controlled grab. They came from the John Barry, *a ship sunk by a torpedo in the Arabian Sea in 1944. Other recent finds have included gold bars and valuable pottery.*

NATURE'S GIFTS

Manganese nodules are found on the seabed below about 2.5 miles (4 km). They contain valuable metals such as copper and nickel and take millions of years to form. Specialized mining systems are being developed to collect them.

Exploring the
DEPTHS

The early films of Hans and Lottie Hass and Jacques Cousteau allowed many people to explore the wonders of the underwater world on their own TV sets. Now, with modern diving suits and camera equipment, ordinary people can plunge into the oceans and examine their watery secrets for themselves. Louis Boutan, the inventor of the first underwater camera, would have been amazed to see the disposable waterproof cameras now for sale. Some resorts now offer submarine trips rather than boat tours. Soon you may be able to buy a submersible of your own!

PRESSURE SUITS
Wearing some diving suits feels like wearing a submarine! The Wasp *and* Jim *(left) are popular designs, in which a diver can reach 1,650 feet (500 m) with enough air for three days. However, the suits are expensive and clumsy to use.*

Do submarines ever get lost?
On September 1, 1973, a small submersible, the *Pisces III*, was rescued from 1,580 feet (480 m) below sea level. Two men had been trapped inside for three days, after losing control of the craft and straying out of radio contact with their surface ship. It took two crewed submersibles and a robot vehicle to find and recover the submarine.

OCEAN FLYERS
Deep Flight One *(above) is a new craft that "flies" underwater. It is very strong, but weighs only as much as a large car. Deep Flight Two may soon take people down to the depths more easily than the clumsy* Trieste.

FISHING THE DEEP

Scientists can catch animals from the deep-sea floor by using special underwater sleds with nets. The sled is towed by a ship over the muddy seabed, on the end of a cable up to 9 miles (15 km) long. It can carry instruments to examine the water, and video or still cameras.

SNAPPING THE OCEANS

Scientists have started dropping their cameras into the sea! The Bathysnap (left) is a special camera that sinks to the seabed and takes pictures of the mysterious animals that live deep down. When the film is finished, the camera is automatically released from the heavy weights which hold it and floats to the surface.

Say "Cheese!"

Louis Boutan took the first underwater photograph in 1893 (left), but his camera was heavy and clumsy. Today's cameras are small and light and have brought many of the ocean's mysteries to life. Special lamps emphasize colors and scenery. Remote-controlled still and video cameras can explore the seabed, sending back images to scientists on research ships. These pictures can be transmitted live to laboratories and museums worldwide.

YELLOW SUBMARINE

The British scientist Robert Leeds has recently designed a small "yellow submarine" (right), shaped like a flying saucer, for commercial use.

It will be tested in 1996 and, if it is declared safe, you may soon be able to hire one and go fish-watching down to a depth of 165 feet (50 m).

"It is true that we are destroying an extraordinary world we scarcely know, almost without thinking. Yet there are many ways to stop this happening...we cannot put off action until tomorrow."

Greenpeace

The Future of the
OCEANS

Our oceans will face all sorts of problems in the future. When the *Exxon Valdez* tanker was wrecked in the Arctic Ocean in 1989, it lost 35,000 tons of oil. Thousands of birds, otters, fish, and shore animals were killed. Every year, 20 billion tons of environmentally damaging substances are dumped into the ocean, while many sea birds, dolphins, and turtles are trapped in nets meant to catch squid, and die. Fish are being taken from the sea faster than they can replace themselves.

However, if we are able to solve these problems, the oceans hold an exciting future for us. Astronauts have lived for up to a year in space. Soon we should be able to do the same in the sea. So far, aquanauts have only lived underwater for a few weeks, but who knows – one day we might build and inhabit underwater cities. Our future may depend upon our oceans. We must look after them.

Inhabiting the OCEANS

People have always dreamed of living underwater. Many fantastic stories have been written about "human fish" and underwater cities. The first steps have been taken toward making this dream come true. Scientists have developed a membrane that keeps water out but allows oxygen to pass in. It has been tried successfully on rabbits. Could it one day allow humans to breathe freely underwater? Divers are already able to live for some time in "underwater homes," or saturation habitats. These are small and cramped but, one day, larger underwater homes may be created, in which people can live and work for many months or even several years.

BREATHING UNDER THE SEA
In the 1960s, scientist Waldemar Ayres used a special membrane to take oxygen from sea water through artificial "gills." He breathed underwater for over an hour. No one has yet used his system for diving.

WATERY HOUSES
The first "underwater home" for divers was the Conshelf I, *invented by Jacques Cousteau. In 1962, two divers spent a week in it at a depth of 33 feet (10 m). Sealab (right) and Tektite are habitats in which people have lived for up to 30 days at depths of nearly 660 feet (200 m).*

AN ICY ENVIRONMENT
Even the cold waters of the Arctic and Antarctic are being explored by diving scientists. They have discovered giant sea spiders, anemones, and fish with antifreeze in their blood.

FARMING THE OCEANS

Many countries have sea farms where fish, shrimps, shellfish, (right), and seaweeds are cultivated for food. At present, these are mostly established in shallow water where they can be looked after easily. One day, it may be possible to farm deep-sea fish with diver-farmers living in underwater farmhouses.

How long can people hold their breath underwater?
Most people can hold their breath for about 30 seconds. In December 1994, Francesco "Pipin" Ferreras became the world breath-holding champion when he dived to 420 feet (127 m). He held his breath for 2 minutes, 26 seconds. **WARNING: THIS IS A VERY DANGEROUS THING TO DO AND SHOULD NOT BE TRIED.**

TAKING THE PLUNGE

Scuba gear means that almost anyone can learn to dive and explore the deep. But compressed air, used by most divers, is unsafe below about 165 feet (50 m).

Special mixtures of the gases nitrogen or helium and oxygen allow trained divers (left) to reach 330 feet (100 m). Below that, divers use a diving bell as a base, to work down to about 1,320 feet (400 m).

Cities of the future

Many books and films have explored the possibilities of humans living underwater in specially designed towns and cities. Already, a few travel agencies are experimenting with submerged hotels (right) from which guests can watch fish, snorkel, and scuba dive. But as the Earth's population increases, will underwater buildings have more serious uses? Will human colonies be able to live in the depths of the oceans?

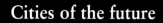

The Unsolved
MYSTERIES

Despite modern ships and scientific equipment, many ocean mysteries remain to be solved. Some, like eel migrations, have been partly explained by observations over many years. Many ancient legends of sea serpents were probably inspired by sightings of rare creatures like the oarfish. Tales of battles between giant sea serpents and whales may be true, because sperm whales eat giant squid. But not all the stories can be explained. Who knows what other creatures may still lurk in the dark depths of the ocean?

A TANGLE OF TENTACLES
When a giant octopus (below) spreads out its arms, you can fit two large cars between them. These huge creatures can be 11.5 feet (3.5 m) long. They are intelligent and shy and are rarely seen; no one knows just how big they can get.

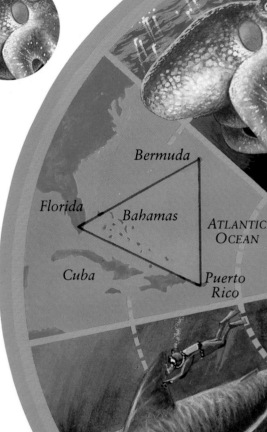

Bermuda

Florida

Bahamas

ATLANTIC
OCEAN

Cuba

Puerto
Rico

WANDERING GIANTS
Every April, huge whale sharks appear off the Australian Barrier Reef. Basking sharks (left) leave the coasts of Europe in the winter, but no one knows where they go. The travels of these giants are being investigated using radio tags linked to

Are octopuses dangerous?
Some kinds are. The pretty blue-ringed octopus, found in Australia, is small – only 5–6 in (10–15 cm) – but its bite can kill a person in just a few minutes.

Octopuses have three hearts, but this does not make them particularly strong. They get tired very quickly and will give up a fight if it is too difficult.

Many marine animals make long migrations, but it is still a mystery how they find their way. People used to believe that the long hairs from a horse's tail turned into young eels

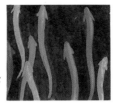

when they dropped into a river. The eels are now known to migrate to rivers for thousands of miles, from the Sargasso Sea (see page 19). How do they find their way? This is still a puzzling secret.

The fearsome Kraken

For centuries, people have told stories of the Kraken – a huge, octopus-like animal which can pull down a ship. These tales are probably based on giant squid, which can be 50 feet (15 m) long. Their tentacles may have been mistaken for sea serpents.

SNAKES ALIVE!

The strange oarfish grows to a staggering 25 feet (7 m) long and lives in deep water. With its bright red fins and "mane," it could be mistaken for a sea serpent.

But some sightings remain unexplained. In 1817, a huge "sea serpent" was seen in Massachusetts by many people over several weeks...but its identity is still a mystery.

THE DEADLY TRIANGLE

Over 70 ships and 20 planes are said to have vanished in the Bermuda Triangle in the Atlantic Ocean. Future searches may find these wrecks and explain their disappearance.

BLOBS ON THE BEACH

In the last century, huge, 5–10-ton "blobs" of dead sea creatures have been washed up worldwide. Could they be parts of unknown giant beasts?

The power of the ocean

As science and technology develop, scientists are able to unravel more and more of the secrets of our oceans. Yet humans still have a long way to go if we are to fully understand this mysterious, dark world ruled by giant monsters and amazing creatures – a world in which we will always be strangers.

TYPVS ORBIS TERRARVM

6th century B.C. Pythagoras
proves Earth is round
c. 5000 B.C. Legends of fish-tailed
goddesses appear
c. 3000 B.C. First records of pearl diving
Ancient Egyptians invent sails
c. 1500 B.C. Volcanic eruption on Santorini
c. 750 B.C. Homer describes Charybdis
c. A.D. **50** Mela draws "wheel map" of Earth
c. 1300 Tortoise-shell goggles used
1520 Magellan discovers Pacific Ocean
1522 Magellan's ship sails around world
1570 Ortelius publishes Theatrum Orbis
Terrarum, *the first world atlas*
1690 Halley invents diving bell
1715 Early diving suit invented
1763 "Leptocephalus" found in Sargasso
Sea and thought to be strange fish
1773 Phipps takes depth sounding
1807 Steamboat invented
1837 Siebe invents helmet diving suit
1860 Life found on Mediterranean cable
1865 Rouquayrol and Denayrouze invent
independent diving set
1872 H.M.S. Challenger *departs on voyage*
1893 Boutan takes undersea photograph
1912 Titanic *sinks*
1915 Pangaea theory proposed
1920 Echo sounders first used
1930 Barton and Beebe's
bathysphere
dive

LINE

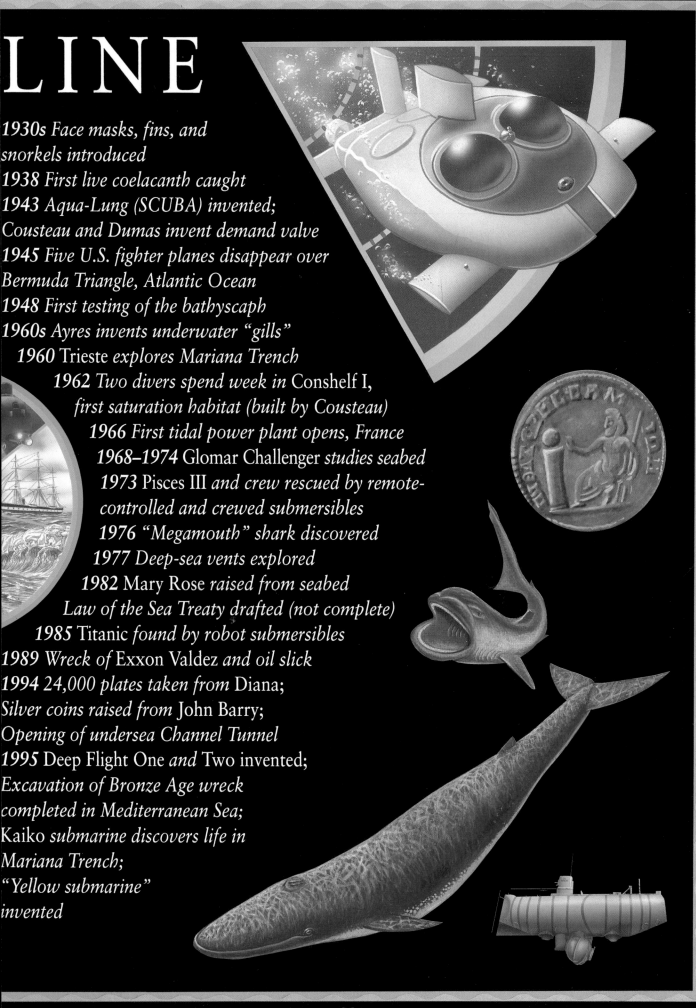

1930s *Face masks, fins, and snorkels introduced*

1938 *First live coelacanth caught*

1943 *Aqua-Lung (SCUBA) invented; Cousteau and Dumas invent demand valve*

1945 *Five U.S. fighter planes disappear over Bermuda Triangle, Atlantic Ocean*

1948 *First testing of the bathyscaph*

1960s *Ayres invents underwater "gills"*

1960 Trieste *explores Mariana Trench*

1962 *Two divers spend week in* Conshelf I, *first saturation habitat (built by Cousteau)*

1966 *First tidal power plant opens, France*

1968–1974 Glomar Challenger *studies seabed*

1973 Pisces III *and crew rescued by remote-controlled and crewed submersibles*

1976 *"Megamouth" shark discovered*

1977 *Deep-sea vents explored*

1982 Mary Rose *raised from seabed Law of the Sea Treaty drafted (not complete)*

1985 Titanic *found by robot submersibles*

1989 *Wreck of* Exxon Valdez *and oil slick*

1994 *24,000 plates taken from* Diana; *Silver coins raised from* John Barry; *Opening of undersea Channel Tunnel*

1995 *Deep Flight One and* Two *invented; Excavation of Bronze Age wreck completed in Mediterranean Sea;* Kaiko *submarine discovers life in Mariana Trench;* "Yellow submarine" *invented*

INDEX

Picture credits (abbreviations: t-top, m-middle, b-bottom, r-right, l-left):
4-5, 25b: Bruce Coleman Ltd; 8-9, 11: Ancient Art & Architecture Collection; 17, 22, 25t, 29, 31, 35, 37: Frank
Spooner Pictures; 28: Spectrum Colour Library